The Banshee Queen of Cork

Oisín McGann
Illustrated by **Derry Dillon**

Published 2014
Poolbeg Press Ltd

123 Grange Hill, Baldoyle
Dublin 13, Ireland

Text © Poolbeg Press Ltd 2014

A catalogue record for this book is available from the British Library.

ISBN 978 1 78199 977 6

Cover design and illustrations by Derry Dillon
Printed by GPS Colour Graphics Ltd Alexander Road, Belfast BT6 9HP

The Banshee Queen of Cork

This book belongs to

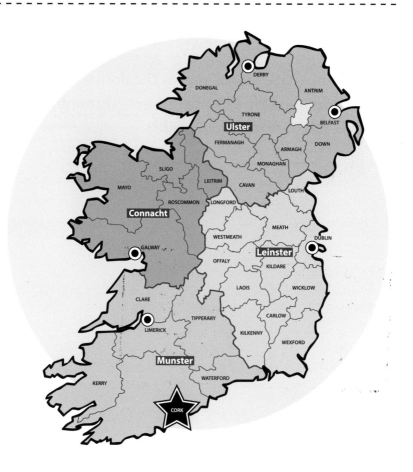

MAC – Mythical Activity Control

Mission Info

There was a time, long ago, when Ireland was a place of magic. Now, all the magical people and creatures live in the Otherworld. To people like you, they are just myths and legends. But sometimes they can escape into your world.

Mythical Activity Control guards the doorways to your world. And when someone gets through, it's MAC's job to bring them back.

From the Agent Files:

ÁINE *(pronounced 'AWN-yeh')*
Ancestor:
Áine, Goddess of
Summer and Light.
Personality:
Smart but stubborn.
Loves nature.
Can judge the moods of
people and animals.
Power:
Can talk to animals.
Can travel through
mirrors and polished metal.

FIONN *(pronounced 'Fy-UNN')*
Ancestor:
Legendary warrior Fionn McCool.
Personality:
Clever, sensible, but curious too
and that can get him into trouble.
Power:
Can connect to information from
either world by biting his thumb,
like his ancestor after he tasted
the Salmon of Knowledge.
Can travel through mirrors and polished metal.

TOGETHER, they help keep you safe from the
wild magic of the Otherworld.

Also in the MAC series

Viking Thunder in Dublin

Coming Soon in the MAC series

Queen Maebh's Raging Return to Galway

The Lord in the Lake in Limerick

ALSO...

It was a shock when she appeared. The rock band were on stage at a place called Charles Fort. It was a huge old fort near Kinsale in County Cork, out by the sea. It was a cloudy, gloomy afternoon, but the band was playing to a huge, happy, dancing crowd. Everyone was having a great time. And then the banshee showed up.

The band was performing one of their biggest hits . . . and then a beautiful woman appeared out of nowhere. She was standing by one of the microphones. The crowd clapped and cheered. They thought the band had performed some kind of magic trick.

But the five musicians stared at the woman.
They didn't know who she was or where she
had come from.

The woman opened her mouth to the microphone as if she was going to join in the singing . . . Then she let out a scream that split the air. People cried out in pain as they covered their ears. The band dropped their instruments and ran off the stage in terror. Then every light bulb in the place smashed and glass tinkled to the ground.

There was a moment of silence. Everyone had a whine in their ears after the deafening scream. The beautiful woman glared out at the people. Some of them were crying, some were just amazed at what they'd seen and heard. Then she gave another screech and disappeared again. The screech seemed to take off and shoot across the fort. It faded into the sky, heading east over the sea.

A few minutes after the woman appeared at the concert, two more people arrived at Charles Fort. There was a big trailer behind the stage. The band used it as a dressing room. The scream had smashed all the mirrors in the dressing room . . . except one. It shimmered and rippled and two children stepped out of it.

Their names were Áine and Fionn. They were secret agents. They worked for MAC – Mythical Activity Control. It was their job to make sure no one from the Otherworld caused trouble in this world. And now someone was.

The band's drummer was sitting in the room when the children appeared. He was in his underwear, hugging an old teddy bear, shivering with fear. When the MAC agents stepped out of the mirror, he squealed and jumped into a wardrobe.

"I think we scared him," Fionn said.

"Ah, he was already scared when we got here," Áine said. "Come on – let's go see what Clíona's been up to. I really don't understand what she's doing here."

Clíona was acting very strangely. In the old days the banshees used to appear, crying and screeching, as a warning that someone was going to die. But they hadn't done that for centuries.

The two children stepped out of the trailer and climbed up the steps to the back of the stage. Everything was dark under the evening sky. Broken glass lay everywhere, from all the smashed light bulbs.

"She made a right old mess, didn't she?" Fionn said quietly.

Áine and Fionn gazed out at the crowd. There were a few hundred people there, but most of them were leaving now.

Áine looked up and saw something. She whistled and a tiny shape flitted down out of the sky towards her. It was a little bat. It squeaked at her and she listened carefully.

Fionn waited while this went on. This was Áine's power: she could talk to animals. And he could tell that this bat was very upset.

"Yes, it must have been very loud," Áine said
to it. "Concerts often are. Yes, it must have hurt
your ears. Can you tell me about the banshee?"
The little bat squeaked again and Áine nodded,
frowning as she listened. She stroked the bat's
head and let it take off, flying away into the
darkness.

"Well?" Fionn asked.

"He said he quite liked the banshee's voice, but the band was awful," she told him.

"I don't think they were playing for bats," Fionn said. "Did he say anything else?"

"Oh, yes, Clíona's headed for Trabolgan holiday camp, east of Cork City – all the other bats are talking about it. He said she looked really angry."

As agents of MAC, Áine and Fionn had to be able to move fast. They had the power to travel instantly through mirrors. They could jump in through a mirror in one place and out through another somewhere else. The mirrors were magical doorways.

It was a lot faster than walking, which was important if you had to chase a powerful banshee like Clíona. She could turn herself into a scream and travel at the speed of sound.

When you knew how to use them, mirrors could even carry you across to the Otherworld. MAC controlled the mirror roads, so the roads obeyed Áine and Fionn's commands. They only had to think of the name of a place, or picture it in their minds and the roads could find the mirror that was nearest to it.

But it's hard to catch a banshee when you're travelling through glass. Áine and Fionn tried to get out through one mirror after another, but they were all broken. Finally, they came to a mirror that was still in one piece and they jumped out of it.

They were in the theatre in Trabolgan holiday camp . . . but they were too late. Children and parents were laughing their heads off at the magician who stood on the stage. The magician was standing there, looking shocked. The glass in his big pair of spectacles was shattered.

"Bet he's wondering how he magicked up a banshee," Áine chuckled.

Fionn bit on his thumb. He had the magical ability to find information in this world, or the Otherworld, by doing this. This time, he was checking the news for reports about the banshee.

"She's moving closer to Cork city," he told Áine, taking the thumb from his mouth. "The chatter on the web says there's trouble at Fota Wildlife Park."

There was a big mirror inside the main entrance of the wildlife park. It trembled and rippled and Áine and Fionn jumped out of it.

They heard the shrieking again. As they raced along one of the roads, they saw animals in a panic. The cheetahs and giraffes were running, the monkeys were covering their heads, the zebras were huddled together.

"What, she's screaming at animals now?" Áine said angrily. "What's going on?"

"There! There she is!" Fionn said.

They saw Clíona standing near a pond. Some peacocks were hiding behind a tree nearby. The banshee looked very upset about something. She raised her face and let out a scream. Then she vanished as if the scream was pulling her into the sky.

"Excuse me!" Áine asked the peacocks. "Do you know where she's going?"

One of the peacocks crowed at her. Áine frowned and looked at Fionn.

"Blarney Castle," she said. "They heard Clíona ask someone for directions to Blarney Castle."

The two MAC agents came out through a tall antique mirror in a grand bedroom in Blarney House, not far from Blarney Castle. They sprinted over to the castle, looking for any sign of Clíona. People were running across the beautiful gardens, away from the castle.

"Another crowd," Áine said. "She's looking for large numbers of people . . . or even animals. But why is she trying to scare them?"

"She was a queen in the Cork area once," Fionn said. "Maybe she wants to take over again."

"Funny way of going about it," Áine snorted. They were standing by the bank of a river. A salmon poked its nose out of the water and gazed up at Áine. She gazed around and saw there were a lot of other fish swimming up close to the riverbank, looking excited.

"That's odd," she said to Fionn. "They're asking where the nice lady went. They liked her voice."

"I can't hear them making any sound," Fionn said, puzzled.

"It's very high-pitched," Áine said. "You need the right ears. Maybe the fish are like the bat. To them, a banshee's scream sounds quite nice."

"But why is she . . .?" Fionn started to say. Then he looked up. "Look! There she is!"

At the top of the castle there was a large
hole just underneath the battlements with bars
across it, and they could see Clíona through the
bars. She was hanging upside down into the
hole. Her long pale hair blew in the wind as
she kissed part of the wall. As the children ran
into the castle, Fionn bit his thumb, looking for
information about the place.

"The Blarney Stone is up there – it's built into the castle wall," he said as they raced up the steps. "People hang backwards off a ledge to kiss it. They say it can make you eloquent."

"What does 'eloquent' mean?" Áine panted, following the narrow, twisting stairs.

"It means you're really good at talking," he replied.

"Why is a banshee worried about being good at talking?" Áine asked, sighing.

"What's that?" Fionn said.

He was looking up at the light at the top of the steep, narrow staircase. He turned around suddenly, blocking Áine's way up the stairs.

"Get back!" he shouted at her. "Get back! Now!"

Clíona stood at the top of the stairs, glaring down at them. She took a deep breath and screamed.

The screech blasted down the tight stone tunnel. It hit Fionn and Áine like an ocean wave. Fionn was blocking Áine and he took the worst of it. It knocked them both backwards down the stairs.

They fell, bouncing painfully down the stone steps. Áine managed to stop them before they fell too far. Fionn groaned, holding his head. He was stunned, hardly able to move.

Áine tried to stand up, and found Clíona standing on the steps just above her. The banshee was looking down at her.

"Stop!" Áine snapped. "Clíona, wait!"

The banshee looked like she was about to scream again, but she stopped.

"The Blarney Stone didn't work," she said. "I'm still the same."

"It's only meant to make you better at talking," Áine told her. "And I don't think it works on banshees. I know why you came here now, from the Otherworld. You didn't want to scare people, did you? And you didn't want to be queen again?"

Clíona shook her head miserably.

"Yeah, I get it now," Fionn said, sitting up as he rubbed his sore head. "You're not screaming . . ."

"You're singing," Áine said. "You just want people to listen to you sing. You want an audience."

"But nobody wants to listen!" Clíona cried, holding up her arms. "They all just run away!"

"I think I have the answer," Áine said. "But we need to get back to the sea."

Mizen Head was a piece of land with towering cliffs looking out at the Atlantic Ocean

It was a wild place, but it had a visitor's centre. There was a mirror in the toilets and Fionn and Áine dived out of it. They crashed right into a woman who was standing there doing her make-up.

"Sorry, sorry!" Fionn said.

The MAC agents ran outside.

Clíona was waiting for them at the top of the cliff. She was already screaming. Or singing, if that's what you wanted to call it. Áine and Fionn covered their ears as they watched the sea. Down in the water, creatures came to the surface. There were all kinds of fish, dolphins and whales, even octopuses and squid. They had all come to hear Clíona sing.

"There's your audience," Áine said, as Clíona went quiet. "Your screaming is music to their ears. They'll do anything for you."

"And there's lots of islands out there with no people," Fionn added, pointing out to sea. "You can find yourself a nice quiet place to perform. If you don't make any more trouble, we won't have to take you back to the Other-world. So what to do you think, Clíona?"

Clíona turned to them, smiled and nodded. Then she looked back at her audience and began screeching again. The creatures of the sea squealed in delight.

"Isn't it nice to see someone so happy?" Áine said softly to Fionn.

He nodded, his hands still over his ears.

"Yes, it is," he said. "Now let's get out of here. She's hurting my head."

And so they left the Banshee Queen of Cork, singing to her fans. And if you're ever down that way, you might still hear her sometimes, singing to the sea.

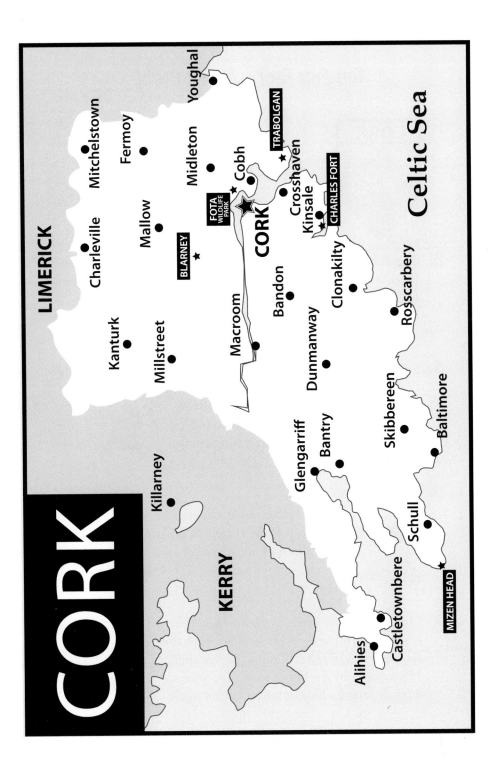

Ten Fun Facts About Cork!

1. Cork Harbour is the second largest in the world, after Sydney Harbour in Australia. Cork's motto is 'A Safe Harbour for Ships'.

2. The name '*Cork*' comes from the Irish '*Corcach*' meaning 'marsh'. Cork was built on islands in the River Lee and its main streets today were river channels until the 18th century, when they were built over. No wonder there's so much flooding there every year!

3. Saint Finbarr founded a monastery in the area in the 7th century. But the city of Cork was founded by the Vikings. They used to raid the monastery but then they began to supply the monks with salt and wine in return for animal hides!

4. Cork's famous landmark, the 'Goldy Fish' weathervane on top of the steeple of St Ann's Shandon Church, is almost 4 metres long.

5. On Cork's main street, Patrick Street, there is a stone drinking trough for dogs, with the Irish word 'MADRAÍ' ('dogs') carved on it. It was made by the famous sculptor Séamus Murphy and he liked it best of all his work.

6. At the top of Blarney Castle near Cork, you can kiss the Blarney Stone, by leaning backwards over a hole in the battlements. Scary! This will give you 'The Gift of the Gab', meaning you'll be a wonderful talker from then on!

7. County Cork invented the kind of horseracing known as 'steeplechasing' in 1752, when one man challenged another to race from the church steeple at Buttevant to the church steeple at Doneraile.

8. Fota Island in Cork Harbour is a wildlife park. Giraffes, zebras, ostriches and kangaroos roam together in 40 acres of grassland while monkeys swing about in the trees.

9. Cobh on Cork Harbour is where the last 123 passengers boarded the doomed liner *Titanic* on its way to America. *The Titanic Experience Cobh* visitors' centre tells their story.

10. Spike Island in Cork Harbour was used in the 17th century to hold thousands of Irish people being sent to the West Indies as slaves. In the 19th century it was used to hold convicts being transported to Australia. And in the 20th century it was a prison for young offenders. There are over 1000 prisoners buried on the small island.

If you enjoyed this book from
Poolbeg why not visit our website:

www.poolbeg.com

and get another book delivered straight
to your home or to a friend's home.

All books despatched within 24 hours.

POOLBEG

Why not join our mailing list
at www.poolbeg.com and get some
fantastic offers, competitions,
author interviews and much more?

@PoolbegBooks